I Like to Read

A Summer Holiday

sterling

Ruby and Ted's summer holiday had just begun. They were very excited as they were going to spend a few days at a hill station.

"Father, we're ready to go," shouted Ruby.

"Yes, our suitcase is packed and ready. What about yours?" said Ted.

"This suitcase just won't shut," panted Father. "Come and help me shut it, children."

The suitcase was packed with woollens. The children sat down on it and bounced up and down, laughing all the while, until Father was able to shut it.

"Whew! That was quite a job. Thank you, children," said Father.

Mother came in and said, "I'm ready now."

"Father, have you packed the camera?" asked Ruby.

"Yes, dear," said Father, as he took the suitcase out to the car.

"Mother, where are the snacks?" asked Ted.

"Jean is just packing them," said Mother. "Why don't you go to the kitchen and help her?"

Jean was their old housekeeper. Ted went into the kitchen and began helping her.

"Don't forget the chips and juice, Jean," said Ted.

"I've already packed them, dear," said Jean with a smile. "Will you miss me, Ted?"

"Oh yes, Jean, I'll miss you. But we'll be back soon," said Ted.

Father put the bags in the boot of the car and they all got in.

"Hooray! We're off at last," shouted Ted, jumping up and down in the back seat.

"How long will it take to reach, Mother?" asked Ruby.

"I'm not sure, but I think it will take about four hours to reach the hill station," said Mother.

They waved a cheerful goodbye to Jean.

"Goodbye, children," said Jean. "Take care and have a nice time."

"Goodbye, Jean, we'll miss you," said the children.

"I'll miss you, too," said Jean as she waved to them. "Make sure you take plenty of photographs of the hill station."

As they drove away, Ted saw his friend Benny on his bicycle.

"Goodbye, Benny, we're going on a summer holiday," he shouted.

"Goodbye, Ted, have a nice time," said Benny. "I shall be going on a holiday next week. I'll see you when you get back."

"Yes," said Ted. "We'll show you photographs of the hill station."

Soon they had left the town far behind. All around them there were fields of corn and wheat. The crops swayed in the breeze.

Ruby rolled down her window and listened to the wind rushing past.

After some time, the children began to feel hungry.

"May we stop for a while and have some snacks?" asked Ted. "I'm hungry."

"Yes. I'm hungry, too," said Ruby.

Father stopped the car near a grassy spot and they took out the snacks.

Jean had packed sandwiches, chips, cake and lemonade. As they ate, they looked around them. A farmer was driving a red tractor in a field nearby.

A bus full of schoolchildren went past them. The schoolchildren waved at Ted and Ruby, and they waved back.

"We're going on a summer holiday," shouted Ruby.

When they had finished eating, Father said, "Children, please help me clear up. Pick up the crumbs and bits of food lying around. We must not litter the place."

"Yes, Father," said the children.

Mother packed the leftover food. The children picked up the crumbs and bits of food. A little bird was hopping around nearby.

"Let's give these crumbs to that little bird," said Ruby. "It must be hungry."

They put the crumbs and bits of food below a tree. The bird flew to it at once and began pecking at the crumbs.

"Isn't it sweet?" said Ruby.

A crow was sitting on that tree. It saw the bird pecking at the crumbs. It flew down and began cawing loudly. The little bird was frightened and flew away.

"Shoo," said Ted, trying to frighten the crow. "Don't take the little bird's food, you greedy crow."

The crow cawed loudly again, flapped its wings and flew straight at Ted.

He got frightened and cried out, "Mother!"

Mother shooed away the crow. Ted covered his face and began to cry.

"Don't cry, Ted. The crow has gone," said Ruby. "Mother has shooed it away."

Mother hugged Ted and took him back to the car.

As they were getting into the car, Mother said to Father, "Let me drive for a while now. Then you can get some rest."

So Father leaned back in his seat, switched on the car radio and shut his eyes.

After a while Ruby said, "Look over there, I can see the mountains!"

"Where?" asked Ted excitedly.

"There," she said, pointing out of the window.

"I want to take some photographs of the mountains," said Father. "Let's stop here for a while."

Mother parked the car on the side of the road. Father got out with the camera and took some photographs. Then they got back into the car.

Soon they had begun climbing the mountain. The road was narrow and winding and the car turned this way and that around the sharp curves. Ruby began to feel sick. There was a funny feeling in her stomach and she had a headache.

"Mother, please stop," she said.

"What is it, dear?" asked Mother, as she stopped the car on the side of the road.

"I feel sick," said Ruby, getting out of the car.

"Walk around for a while. You'll feel better," said Father.

Mother gave her a tablet.

"Here, take this tablet, dear. It's for mountain sickness," she said.

Ruby took the tablet and then splashed some cold water on her face and neck.

"I feel better now," she said.

They got back into the car and Mother took care to drive slowly.

They passed a school. Little children in colourful clothes were playing in the playground. Mother stopped the car near the school. Ruby got down with the camera and took some photographs.

They reached the hill station around noon. Their hotel faced the valley.

The children got out and looked around them.

"It's so beautiful," said Ruby.

"And so quiet. You can even hear the wind in the trees," said Mother, as she got out.

"I am hungry again," said Ted.

"But you just ate some time ago," said Ruby.

"Mountain air makes us hungry more often," said Mother with a smile. "Now help us take the bags to the rooms."

As soon as they had put away their bags in their rooms, Ted ran out to the playground.

"Ted, I thought you were hungry," said Mother.

"I'll play for some time and then eat," he called out. "Coming, Ruby?"

"I'll just have a wash and come," said Ruby.

She washed her face and hands. Then she ran out to the playground.

"What shall we play?" asked Ruby.

"Look, here's a swing!" said Ted.

Ted and Ruby played on the swing for a while. Then they found a rubber ball and began playing with it.

"Here, Ted, catch," said Ruby, as she threw the ball.

But Ted could not catch the ball. It bounced down the side of the mountain.

"There, now it's lost," said Ruby.

They went to the edge of the mountain and looked down.

"Look! There's the ball. It's bouncing past those bushes," said Ted.

A village boy had been watching them play. He saw the ball bouncing down. He ran down the side of the mountain, searched among the bushes and got the ball out.

"Thank you," said Ruby and Ted, as he handed them the ball.

"What's your name?" asked Ted.

"Joe," said the boy shyly.

"Please come and play with us tomorrow," said Ruby. "We will be staying here for a few days. It will be nice to have someone to play with."

The boy nodded his head, smiled shyly and ran away.

Every morning Ted and Ruby played in the playground till their mother and father got ready. After that, all of them went for long walks along the narrow mountain roads.

Ruby loved the wild flowers growing on the side of the mountain. Every day, she picked a bunch of them and put them in a vase in her room.

One day, when Ruby was plucking some wild flowers, she touched a leaf and her hands began to itch.

"Oh Mother," she cried. "My hands are itching and hurting."

A villager was passing by. He quickly plucked a leaf from a nearby tree.

"Here, rub this leaf on your hands. They will stop itching," he said.

Ruby rubbed the leaf and felt better at once.

"Thank you," she said.

Mother and Father thanked the villager too.

"You must be careful while plucking wild flowers," said the villager, and went away.

Sometimes, they walked to the village. There they watched the villagers doing their daily work.

The village boy soon became good friends with Ruby and Ted. Every day, he brought along a few of his friends and all the children played together.

The village children showed Ruby and Ted how to climb trees and pluck juicy fruit.

"This is fun," Ruby said. "We must show our friends back home how to climb trees."

One day, Mother and Father took Ruby and Ted to the village handicraft shop where they bought gifts for their grandparents, for Jean and their friends.

"Let's buy these caps for Benny and Susie," said Ted.

"Yes, they are nice," Ruby said. Father bought a belt for Grandpa. Mother bought a blouse for Grandma and a scarf for Jean.

They also took some photographs of the village and the friends they had made there.

The days flew past. Soon it was time to go back home.

On the drive back home, everyone was very quiet. They were sad that their holiday had come to an end.

But when they reached home, the children rushed to Jean and began to tell her all about their holiday.

"Look, Jean, here's the scarf Mother bought for you," said Ruby. "Isn't it pretty?"

"Yes, it is. Thank you so much," said Jean.

The children spent the rest of their holidays telling their friends about the wonderful time they had at the hill station.

They showed them the photographs and told them about the friends they had made in the village.

"I shall never forget this lovely holiday," said Ruby.

"Mother, can we go back there again next year?" said Ted.

"We'll see, dear," said Mother with a smile.

How did the children
shut the suitcase?